# Fenn's
# Bells

**Heavenly Realm Publishing**
*Houston, Texas*

# Reed Randall

Published & Printed by,
Heavenly Realm Publishing
1-866-216-0696

Visit our Website at: www.heavenlyrealmpublishing.com
               shop.heavenlyrealmpublishing.com


Printed in the United States of America

ISBN—13- 9781944383183 (paperback)
ISBN—13- 9781944383190 (hardback)

Library of Congress Control Number: 2020915438


1. FICTION / Mystery & Detective / General: *Fenn's Bells* / 2. RELIGION / General: *Fenn's Bells* / 3. FICTION / General: *Fenn's Bells* / Reed Randall

This book is printed on acid free paper.

# Table of Contents

*Letter* ................................................................................ 4

*Preface* ............................................................................. 5

**Chapter 1:** House Calls ..................................................... 9

**Chapter 2:** Title to the Gold ......................................... 15

**Chapter 3:** The Drawing ................................................. 21

**Chapter 4:** Zodiac Sign ................................................... 25

**Chapter 5:** The Adventure Begins ................................ 33

**Chapter 6:** Highway Thirteen ....................................... 37

**Chapter 7:** Lonely Thoughts ......................................... 49

**Chapter 8:** Stone Marker ............................................... 57

**Chapter 9:** Valley of Death ........................................... 65

**Chapter 10:** Easter Sunday ............................................ 71

**Chapter 11:** Directions ................................................... 77

**Chapter 12:** Finding the Bells ....................................... 83

**Chapter 13:** Headed Home ............................................. 91

*Closure* ........................................................................... 93

*Conclusion* .................................................................... 109

*Dear Forrest Fenn*

*I wanted to thank you again for the blessing that have passed on to me and my family. I don't know how you were able to pull this off, or even knew it would possibly work, but it did.*

*You have left so many people wondering about the finale, and many of them are still trying to find your WWWH. And I think it is hilarious, how much more of this story there really is. For now, I will give the world your Blaze that they have all been searching for. And when the time is right, I will tell them what was really in the chest that no one knew.*

*I am sure you are aware that Anna came to me while I was sleeping and told me that time is no longer of value. And I knew that I needed to get back to the waterfall and begin preparing everything for your arrival.*

*Forrest, many people will travel to verify that this story is real. I am sure that eventually, everyone will finally understand what this was all about. But until then, I will keep my promise that I made to you that night, and this will be our little SECRET!*

*Sincerely,*

*Reed "Ophiuchus" Randall*

*The Finder*

# *Preface*

Finally, home and the chase is over. I have succeeded in the one goal that I had set out to do, and that was to find Forrest Fenn's treasure, which I did.

I am sitting here on the edge of my bed, with a huge smile on my face, knowing that I was the one to find Fenn's Treasure. Never in a million years did I imagine achieving something so amazing and fantastic, but to be the one to break Fenn's Code, has been a thrill.

It has taken me a little less than a year to find the Blaze and make sense of everything, almost as if a higher power had sent me on a mission to help recover the truth about the treasure hunt. Actually, I am pretty sure Fenn didn't think anyone would be able to understand his cryptic book or maybe he did? But for some reason, I knew exactly what he was trying to say the very first time I read the poem.

If you're still wondering, how is it that I was able to understand what Forrest was thinking, when there were half a million other searchers out there looking for the same treasure chest, and I had to be the one to have discovered his infamous treasure? Well prepare yourself for a story that you would never believe, because this adventure has been more of a thrill than it has been a chase. During this adventure, I met many people along the way, some living and some not so living.

Forrest didn't tell anyone the truth behind his Treasure Hunt. Sorry I mean, he didn't tell any of the searchers that there was the possibility that they may encounter a few unexpected guests along the way. Neither did he explain what it really means when you actually cross the vale.

This is a true story about how I was called into action from the man upstairs, to venture into the valley of darkness and sacrifice my own life, to uncover the truth about the treasure and to find out Fenn's Secret. In the process, I learned about a very special person along the way, and that is myself. I discovered more about myself that I didn't know before this treasure hunt had come into my life. One of the greatest things that I learned about myself during this adventure, is that I am not afraid. And I had to travel through the door of darkness, only to be able to come back to tell you the real story of The Thrill of the Chase.

# Fenn's
# Bells

# CHAPTER ONE

## House Calls

ood morning doctor, thanks again for coming over to check on my mom." Jake said as he opened the door for Dr. Greene.

"Morning Jake, how is she doing today?"

Dr. Greene places his medical bag on the kitchen table and looks around the cluttered room. He could tell that no one had been in that room in a while.

"Do you have any more coffee left? I had another house call this morning and I'm already running low on caffeine." Dr. Greene says as he walks towards the kitchen area.

"Well it's your lucky day, I just made a fresh pot right before you got here." Jake says as he heads towards the sink, to get Dr. Greene a coffee cup. "How do you like your coffee?"

"One cream, one sugar will be great."

"Hey Doc, do you think that we can change my mom's medicine? She's starting to break out in hives on her arms. I think she may be allergic to the medicine."

"Let me go check on her really quick, I'll get that coffee on the way out." Dr. Greene announces from across the room, as he walks towards Mrs. Blanding's bedroom.

Dr. Greene knocks quietly on the bedroom door before hearing a low voice telling him to come in.

"Good morning, how are you feeling today?"

Mrs. Blanding sitting up in her bed staring out the window. As the Dr. enters her bedroom, the lights were dim, but the curtains were drawn open to allow the sun to shine into the bedroom. Mrs. Blanding still staring out the window, "I don't know why my son called you, I told him that I was fine and not to bother you."

"You're not bothering me one bit. I look forward to seeing your pretty face." Dr. Greene says in a joking manner. "Can I take a look at your arms, and see what's going on?"

Dr. Greene reaches over to Mrs. Blanding's hand to get a closer look at her arm. He notices several red spots all the way down to her elbow. "Looks like we may have to change your medicine again. How long have you had this rash?"

"Only a few weeks, but it's no big deal. I don't know why my son is making such a big deal out of this?" Mrs. Blanding turns her head back towards the small window, in the corner of her room. Then she mumbles, "He has other stuff to worry about besides me."

Dr. Greene's phone starts to ring as he steps away from the bed to answer the call. He is standing on the other side of the room, quietly talking to someone on the phone for a few seconds, before hanging up.

"Mrs. Blanding, I have to run. This evening I'll send over your prescription to the pharmacy, and I hope you start feeling better soon. If you need anything else, just let me know." Dr. Greene says as he opens the door to exit the bedroom. Mrs. Blanding was still staring out her bedroom window, as the doctor exits the room.

In the kitchen, Jake was still standing there drinking a cup of coffee and picking up the dishes from the breakfast table. "Jake, I have to take a rain check on that coffee, I need to run by the house really quick, but as soon as I get back to the office, I'll call the pharmacy so they can start your mom's prescription." Jake looks over towards the Dr. and says, "Thanks again for stopping by, and if there is anything that I can do for you, please just let me know."

"I will keep that in mine, talk soon."

"Drive safe!"

Dr. Greene grabs his bag from the dining room table and rushes out the door and says, "I will thank you."

Before he has a chance to start his truck, Dr. Greene pulls his phone out, to call his wife back, to find out what the emergency was.

"Hey, what's going on?" asks Dr. Greene.

"I'm not sure what is going on, but you need to come home now!" Dr. Greene's wife says, "The police are here with a search warrant, and they are going through all of our stuff.  Why are they here, what's going on?"

"I don't know, but I am on my way home now!"

Pulling up to his house, it looked like a scene from the movies.  Police vehicles were parked on both sides of the street. There was an officer standing in the middle of the road directing traffic.  Snipers were even set up across the street, stationed on top of the roof of the neighbor's house.

Dr. Greene pulls up to the officer directing traffic and asks, "What's going on? I live here."
The officer steps back from the window and draws her service pistol and says, "Turn the vehicle off, and get out slowly.  Put your hands behind your head. You are under arrest."

"What's going on, what is this all about?"  Dr. Greene yells at the officer, as he gets out of his vehicle.

"Hands on the back of your head." The officer said, as her partner walked up to assist with the arrest.  "Dr. Greene, you have the right to remain silent, and anything you say, can be held against you in the court of law.  You have the right to talk to a lawyer.  If you cannot afford a lawyer, one will be appointed for you. Do you understand your rights?"

"Where is my wife?"

The officer says, "She is fine, we need you to come with us, and someone will be with you in just a minute."  Several minutes later another officer walked over to the vehicle, where Dr. Greene was sitting handcuffed in the back of a police vehicle.

"Dr. Greene, do you know why you are under arrest?"

"No I don't."

"You're under arrest for illegal possession of tribal artifacts, which is a felony."

Dr. Greene looks out the side window of the police cruiser and sees his wife sitting in the driveway crying, as a female officer stands over her with a note pad asking her questions. "Why is this happening? I have never done anything wrong, ever. This is a huge mistake!"

A few weeks later, Dr. Greene's wife found him dead in his office, from a gunshot wound. And sitting on his desk, was a note to his wife, that read:

*Dear Carroll,*

*I am sorry that it has come to this. So much has happened, and I don't understand how things have gotten to this point. I wish that I were strong enough. Tell the kids that I do love them, and never stop believing in me.*

*I Love You!*
*Dr. Joseph E Greene*

# CHAPTER TWO

## *Title to the Gold*

This night was different than the others. The wind was much calmer, the trees around me were not making a sound, and I was alone hundreds of miles away from the place that I called home. Sitting there knowing that I was about to make the biggest decision in my life. As scared as I was, something told me to get out of this car, and go answer the call.

As the wind slowly started picking up outside of my rental car, the trees in front of me started waving me to get out and come see. I still did not know why I had been called to this empty place, nor did I really know what this was all about. But whatever it was, I was soon about to find out.

The fear of dying is one of the hardest pills that a person will ever have to swallow, but in the end, it is the path that we must all travel, when we finally make that last call home.

I sat there contemplating what to do next, something inside of me was saying let me out. Whatever it was that I had eaten, was ready to explode, and there was no holding back. Something inside of me was trying to come out faster than I could get my belt unbuckled. Never in my life, has this ever happened to me. After a few minutes of throwing up on the side of the rental car, I took another shot of whiskey to get the taste of vomit out of my mouth.

Standing there with my back to the moon and my insides a few feet away, it was time to answer that call that I was too scared to do before. With my back to the moon facing north, I stood there watching my shadow for a few minutes, wondering if this really was my time to go or if I was already dead and just had to face my past.

After a few minutes and a long prayer, it was time, to finalize the deal, and accept my fate. I could still feel the moon calling me, telling me to turn around. With a deep breath and another swig of my whiskey, I turned around to see the moon directly in front of me. Something was there staring down into my soul, just watching me.

"I am here! Why have you called me to this place, what is it that you are trying to show me?" I took a second to have me one more swig just in case it was my last drink. "Whatever you are trying to tell me, I am listening. I know who I am, and I know what this is about!"

There was no one around for miles away, no one close enough to hear me yelling at the moon. The only thing that could hear me, was the trees blowing in the wind, and the water falling from that beautiful waterfall.

"I am not walking away without a fight. So, if you want me, then you're gonna' have to come down here and show me your face!" After a few minutes of staring into that moon, I could feel someone putting their hand on my left shoulder, whispering into my ear to turn around. Lucky for me, I just emptied myself out earlier, because at that moment, I wanted to shit on myself. That's how scared I was.

I took a big swallow of whatever whiskey was left and prepared myself to die. When I turned around, no one was standing anywhere around me. The only thing that was moving, was the small trees that were a few feet in front of me.

A few seconds had passed, and I still didn't see anyone. I decided to look down to make sure that my shadow was still there to show me that I was still alive. And I was, but I wasn't alone. Someone or something was standing there next to me, holding something in its hand. We were standing there, with our backs to the moon, and I could see the shadow raising its hand towards me. As if it was wanting me to accept the gift, and I did. It was the key to unlock the truth about this Treasure Hunt.

After a few minutes, I felt the moon starting to move further away from me, and to my right, the sky was starting to turn orange on the other side of the mountains. It was the beginning of a new day, and within those few minutes, I felt something inside of me that I can't explain, but I will try.

That morning, I headed back to the airport, trying to wrap my mind around what really happened underneath that moon. So much I did not understand, until it finally hit me, that I had found Fenn's Bells. "*I found Fenn's*

*Bells,*" I screamed at the top of my lungs while driving through Hayden. I knew exactly where he hid his bells, and some were in MayBELL, Colorado.

Once I realized the words that came out of my mouth, I pulled the car over immediately. So many emotions started running through my body and tears started pouring from my eyes. I have finally figured out everything that there was to know about Fenn's treasure hunt. While sitting there on the side of the road, crying like a baby, I started to realize what had happened. The bells that no one was looking for was only a riddle. So many emotions were running through me that I could not even think straight. I needed to get out of the car and get as much fresh air as possible before I passed out. On the side of the road, I decided to call my wife, to let her know what happened. I could not tell her everything, because some secrets needed to remain secrets. But I did tell her that my venture was over, and that I am finally coming home.

Almost to the airport, when I looked up to make sure I took the right exit when the numbers came into my head. Exit 272 & 274, that was how many times Fenn climbed that ladder that brought him home, during his experience in the military. The last riddle of the book that I could not figure out, was finally solved. Now I finally knew every riddle and every clue that Fenn wanted me to solve. It was done, the treasure hunt was over.

My flight was leaving out in ninety minutes, and my body was finally able to relax, but something took control of the wheel as I continued driving east. Suddenly the waterfall flashed back into my head, there was something familiar about the other shadow that I recognized. I knew exactly who it was.

When I finally snapped out of that dream, I was twenty miles past my exit and I knew I was in trouble because it was the last flight to Houston for the day, and I had to be back at work in the morning. Now, with time running out, I am racing to get back to the airport before my plane takes off without me. My little rental car was being pushed to its max, and she was giving me everything she could.

As soon as I turned into the rental car lot, I grabbed my bag and ran to the shuttle and handed the driver a $20.00 bill and said, "I need to get to the airport fast!" The shuttle driver told me to buckle up, and then we were off.

The moment the shuttle stopped, I ran as fast as I could to the check-in counter. By the time I handed the lady my driver's license, I was out of breath.

"Mr. Randall, are you okay?" she asked.

"Yes, I don't want to miss my flight."

"Well, it's your lucky day, your flight has been delayed about sixteen minutes." she said as she handed me back my license. As I stood there trying to catch my breath, I felt a lot better knowing that I would be headed home soon.

It had been a long drive and I needed a drink because I still could not believe everything that had happened to me the past couple of days. After security, I stopped at the first bar I saw, and told the bartender to make me a whiskey double.

As I sat there drinking my whiskey and waiting for my meal, I noticed a few more travelers not wearing mask or gloves. People were starting to realize that this corona virus was something that they couldn't control, the virus was going to spread no matter what.

*Last call for flight 1216 leaving for Houston* came over the intercom. That was my cue that I needed to get to my gate before I missed the last flight of the day going home. I asked the bartender for my bill, and she brought me two tickets that were the same, almost identical. I questioned her as to why I had two separate tickets and she explained that she had already closed out my drink ticket before I had ordered my meal.

How crazy was it that both of tickets came out to be $16.20? I could not believe my luck. I really wished that I had bought a lottery ticket, because this had turned into my lucky day.

# CHAPTER THREE

## *The Drawing*

The call came in on 12/20/2001. And I was not quite ready for what was about to happen. I remember standing there at **Cooperfield** Liquor Store, with my usual things, beer, cigarettes and my lucky numbers. On my way into the store, I noticed a camera crew standing around in the parking lot, and a few others were looking down at their phones. I asked the cashier, "What's going on outside, why is the camera crew out there?"

The cashier responded, "Tonight, is the final night to claim the prize, it is the last night, for the winner to come forward with the winning ticket and claim the 13 Million Dollars."

I started thinking to myself, wow I am standing in the same store that someone bought a winning ticket. And I thought, how cool would it be to win 13 Million Dollars.

I asked the cashier if I could see the winning numbers for that day. He had a few extra slips sitting by the register, and he pointed down for me to grab one. While looking at the tickets, I noticed a lot of similarities of the numbers, they were almost identical to the same numbers that I played each week. Eventually I realized that those were in fact my numbers, that I had been playing for the past year. I couldn't believe that I was the lucky winner; I won the Texas Lotto!

And I knew exactly where it was at my mother's house, in a brown cardboard box underneath my bed. The same place where I kept all my other secrets, inside that box. And the killing part about it was, there was only a few hours left until midnight before the ticket becomes worthless. I was running out of time, and I knew that I needed to act fast, if I was going to be the next millionaire.

In no time, I was driving as fast as I could back to my mother's house to go find that ticket. I must have been driving 70 miles an hour, in the neighborhood and my heart was beating a thousand miles an hour. I was so excited this was the big break that I needed to take care of my two daughters and pay for my college admission.

There I was standing in front of that beautiful box, looking at all of the Lotto tickets that I had bought over the past few months, and I knew that inside of that box, was my winning ticket, but I needed to find the right one to be the winner. But there was only one problem, the clock was still ticking, and time was slowly running out.

I felt my heart racing, as I started removing tickets from the box and laying them out neatly on the side of my bed. I distinctly remember being there on June 23rd, because I had just moved back into my mom's house so that I could save up enough money before the semester started. And I remembered the clerk telling me that I had picked too many numbers and needed to decide which one to remove. After a few seconds, I chose to stay with the number sixteen.

After the last ticket was removed from the box, I double checked to make sure there were no stragglers left behind that got overlooked. I started a pile of tickets for the month of June, all others were stacked in a separate pile and placed at the foot of my bed. But I did not want to throw them away just yet in case a few of them were somehow stuck together. There must have been about five or six tickets for June laid out in the middle of my bed, all showing the winning numbers, but I did not see a ticket for June 23rd.

By eleven o'clock, I must have made about three or four trips to the car, checking to see if I had misplaced the ticket in there. Hoping to get lucky, I tried the box one more time just in case I overlooked it by mistake. The ticking of the clock started to get louder and moving faster, my mind was not thinking clearly anymore because by 11:45pm, I had already torn my room apart and pulled everything out of the closet searching for that ticket.

Then it happened, the clock struck midnight, and everything just went silent. No more sounds of the ticks from the clock. No more sounds from the ceiling fan, just above my head. It was just complete silence in my bedroom as I stood there realizing that I had lost thirteen million dollars, just like that.

I needed a drink because my stomach was starting to boil over. But it was after midnight, and I had left my bottle sitting on the countertop when I ran out of the store. That night, I must have laid in the driveway for hours trying to understand why this had to happen to me.

# CHAPTER FOUR

## Zodiac Sign

It has been twenty years since the thirteen-million-dollar dream. And sometimes, I still have to pinch myself to make sure I am still alive. Now looking back on my life, I think that I am in a better place because of not finding that winning lotto ticket. Because really what would a twenty-three-year-old have done with that type of money?

People say that money is the root of all evil, and the older I get, the more I am starting to agree with those people. But my life, has turned out awesome since then. I have accomplished a lot of things without that money. One of my biggest accomplishments was earning my bachelor's degree from University of Houston, even while married and having four kids. After college, I landed a great job with one of the biggest companies in the world, and even learned how to do a few other things as well.

Now that I am at home, I have to start getting things around the house cleaned up because my kids didn't bother trying to clean up after themselves, nor did they check the mail to see if any bills were due. That evening while sitting in my office, that is located next to the kitchen, I could hear my son rummaging through the refrigerator looking for something to eat.

"Hey David, what are you doing?" I screamed through my office door. "I have some food in my bag if you are hungry."

A few seconds later, he opened my office door. "I found some ramen, but we do need to go grocery shopping, because we are out of food."

"I know, we are going tomorrow. How has everything been going around here? Have you been helping your sister out, like I asked you to?"

"It's been boring around here, and I can't really go anywhere because most of my friend's parents won't let them have company over." he said as we both started walking towards the kitchen.

"Look, I know that I have been working for a while, but I am home now, so hopefully things will get back to normal again. How about tomorrow morning we go grocery shopping together, so that you can get out of the house for a little bit and we can get everything we need for our camping trip?"

By this time, he was already pulling his dinner out of the microwave and coming to sit down with me at the dining room table. "Yea, because it's been almost three weeks since I've left this house, and I know how you get when you go grocery shopping."

I looked over at him and said, "What does that mean?"

"Dad, you know how you act! If someone is walking slow in front of you, you get frustrated and then you are ready to leave the store."

"Yeah your right, I'll try and work on that."

"Can we get spaghetti?"

"I don't see why not, as long as you are cooking."

A few minutes later, I could hear my phone ringing from my office and looked over at my son, as he started sucking the juice from his noodles.

"Give me a second I'll be right back!" I said as I headed towards my office. As I made my way around to my desk, to look at my phone, I saw a number that I had seen before, but didn't recognize the caller. By the time my mind registered to answer the phone, the caller had already hung up. Whoever it was I figured they would leave a message and I will call them back tomorrow. Plus, I had some studying to do, because my book, *"The Thrill of The Chase"* just came in, and I wanted to make sure that our first treasure hunt adventure wasn't a complete bust.

After a few minutes of reading the poem, I decided that I would do some research to see what this treasure hunt was all about. Within minutes, I had found a YouTube video where there was this old man named Forrest Fenn, who was saying to marry the poem to a map, and that if you have followed everything correctly, then you would find a chest filled with riches and gold.

This sounded like the perfect adventure for my son and I before he turned 16. A few days later, I decided to look into the poem a little deeper. I spent several hours that night, reviewing google maps and the poem. And by the third night, I had a pretty good place picked out, that I wanted to search, and that was Browns Park, in northwest Colorado.

My son and I both were looking forward to this trip, maybe him more than me. Because most of his life he had been surrounded by women, and up until this point, we haven't done many things together.

Sitting in my office, I started reading through a few of the chapters, looking for clues. And one of the clues that I had picked up on early, was how Forrest Fenn referred to the waterfall as magical. I thought to myself, what's so magical about this waterfall?

By this time, I was curious to know if Browns Park had a waterfall near the park, and it did. Vermillion Waterfalls is one of the sites that is listed as a must see in Browns Park. Along with a few other places, the waterfall is the location that I think the treasure is located.

While reading through my new book, I noticed that he had mentioned July 13, 1956, in the chapter, "My War For Me." And something about that day rang a bell, but I didn't know exactly what it was. Without hesitation, I decided that I would look up the 13th of July, to see what happened that day. And the first thing that popped up on Google was the zodiac sign for cancer.

I started wondering if this was a clue, because Mr. Fenn had at one time in his life suffered with cancer. But after further reading, I noticed that he said, "thirteen to be exact..." Thirteen, but I thought there was only twelve zodiac signs, to be exact.

That night, while researching zodiac signs, I realized that there are thirteen Zodiac signs. And over the last ten years, Astrologers have started reviewing the thirteenth zodiac sign, Ophiuchus. Recently astrologers have started recognizing that the sun has shifted from its normal course of travel, and by this process, it has raised many questions with astrologers. For so many years, I had assumed that I was a Sagittarius, only because it was the only sign listed for my date of birth. And then to find out that I am really an Ophiuchan, by the new zodiac calendars that the Astrologers are working on.

Astrologers are commonly known as people who study zodiac signs, they believe that our destiny lies within the stars. And since the sun now travels in a different elliptical path, as it did 2000 years ago, astrologers have begun taking a closer look at the thirteenth zodiac.

According to Greek mythology, Ophiuchus was a man called Asciepius. He was the son of Apollo and Coronis. Asciepius' mother, Coronis, was a Thessalian princess and lover of Apollo. During her pregnancy, she had fallen in love with a mortal man named Ischys, son of Elatus.

While her husband, Apollo was away performing his duties, he had appointed a white raven to watch over his Coronis, to keep her safe, while he was away. The raven learned of the affair between Coronis and the mortal, and immediately informed Apollo of the situation. Out of anger Apollo killed Ischys, and then turned the raven black as punishment for being a snitch, as well as failing to perform its duties as a protector.

Apollo was infuriated with the information that he had received, that he went to his sister, Artemis, to confide in her about the affair. Artemis, Apollo's sister, killed Coronis with her arrows for the disrespect that she had shown towards the family. Coronis begged for mercy and asked Artemis to spare her unborn child. Apollo attempts to heal Coronis so that his unborn child does not have to suffer in vain for the sins of his mother. But after several failed attempts to save the princess, Apollo chose to cut the unborn baby from the umbilical cord and named the child Asclepius, after his mother Aegle.

As a child, he was given milk by one of the goats that pastured in the valleys of the mountains and was protected by the watch dog of the herd. Apollo entrusted his son to a wise centaur named Chiron, who trained Asclepius to hunt as well as the arts of medicine and healing. Asclepius, known today as Ophiuchus, became so skilled in his studies, that not only could he save lives, but he could also raise the dead.

Glaucus, the young son of King Minos, fell into a jar of honey and drowned. Asclepius watched over the dead body, as a snake had slithered towards the body to resurrect Glaucus. But Asclepius not knowing the snake's real intentions, decided to kill the snake with his staff; then after a few minutes, another snake appeared with an herb in its mouth. The snake placed the herb on the dead snake, and within moments, the dead came back to life.

Asclepius realized the magic that he had witnessed, so he decided to use the same herb, on the body of Glaucus, the son of King Minos, and he too was magically resurrected. Because of this incident, Hades, the god of the Underworld became aware of Asclepius and his powers and realized that the flow of the dead souls into his domain would soon become vain.

Hades began complaining to his brother Zeus, that if Asclepius continues this technique, his kingdom would be in jeopardy if the secret were ever to be told to the others. Zeus, the king of the gods, took his finest lightning bolt and struck Asclepius to death.

Apollo became so angry with Zeus for killing his son, that he took revenge by killing the three Cyclopes who had forged the lightning bolts, that took his sons life. To appease the anger of Apollo, Zeus made Asclepius immortal and set him amongst the other stars in the constellation.

Although Asclepius, known as Ophiuchus, is not one of the official 12 constellations, the Sun passes through its regions the first half of December. The sun's path, the ecliptic, is the black-and-white curved lines crossing the feet of Ophiuchus. The sun also spends more time in Ophiuchus than it does with Scorpius. Therefore, Ophiuchus is referred to as the Thirteenth zodiac sign.

People born under the sign, Ophiuchus, are also referred to as Ophiuchans. Ophiuchans are known to progress well throughout their lives and can sometimes be considered dreamers. Meaning that they can interpret dreams and understand its real meaning. Ophiuchans are also believed to be seekers of wisdom and knowledge and will stop at nothing to learn the truth.

Anyone born under the sign of Ophiuchus, their birthdays will lie at the end of November and beginning of December and the most influential of this sign is believed to have been born on the Thirteenth of December.

As I sat there at my desk thinking about everything that I just read about Ophiuchus, I started to realize that the thirteenth zodiac sign describes me ten times better than the sign of a Sagittarian. This Ophiuchus character seems more along the line of who I really am. And since my birthday is on the Thirteenth of December, I am no longer a Sagittarian, I am an Ophiuchan.

# CHAPTER FIVE

## *The Adventure Begins*

**T**he next evening while sitting at work, I kept thinking about Fenn's poem. Throughout the night, I would glance over at my phone, trying to remember every word of it in the back of my head. Then suddenly, I screamed, "I know where the treasure is!" My other coworkers started laughing, saying there is no way I could have figured it out that quick.

That evening while reading his Memoir, I realized how many clues he was leaving in his book but needed more time to make sense of everything that I had read. Also, my son was super excited, because the past few years has been nothing but work for me, and he was ready for a little guy time away from the women.

We had our date marked for July 13$^{th}$, for us to be packed and on the road, headed out of town. And as a birthday gift, I bought him 2 brand new fishing poles because I knew he loved fishing, and this trip was my way of reeling him in. On the morning of the 13$^{th}$, we were packed and ready to roll.

All we needed now was some breakfast and coffee before our adventure could completely start.

Our first stop was Amarillo, Texas, we stopped at The Big Texan Steak Ranch, home of the 72oz steak, where we feasted on the biggest steaks we had ever seen. The meal was excellent, we enjoyed watching the staff walking around in their cowboy boots and western outfits. After dinner, we walked around for a few minutes before deciding to continue our destination west to New Mexico.

After about another *twenty* minutes on the road, we decided it was time to call it a night and checked in to the Candlewood Suites, off of I-40, in Amarillo. The hotel was exactly what we needed, a warm bed, hot shower and a cold air conditioner. It was perfect, because I knew that this may be the last time that I would be able to sleep in a comfy bed for the next week or so, so I needed to make the best of it.

The next morning, we continued our journey west towards New Mexico. While we were driving, I looked at the map on my phone, and decided on a shortcut that would save us about *twenty* minutes or so of drive time.

And you would not believe what happened next!

As we turned north onto a county road 104, thinking we were going to free up a lot of time by bypassing Albuquerque and Santa Fe, New Mexico. It felt like we drove into a horror movie with no internet, and the fuel light coming on.

After about *twelve miles* into our trip, I became worried that we were not going to make it out of this place alive. There were no houses, no cars passing us by, and on top of everything else, not a single gas station for the next one hundred miles. I was worried to the point that I wanted to turn around, but I didn't want my son to see the fear in my eyes. About an hour later, we saw our first car drive right past us, it was two old ladies, headed the opposite direction. But it helped to relieve some stress, because I was unsure of the direction we were headed, and how much farther we needed to go before getting to town.

We finally arrived in a town called Las Vegas, New Mexico, and the moment I got out of the truck, I dropped down to the ground and kissed the concrete at the gas station because my truck was only showing eighteen miles until empty, and I wanted to cry because of how happy I was seeing real people.

After fueling up with diesel and getting us something to drink, we continued our adventure into Colorado. I knew the directions, but I continued to look down at my map because I didn't want to find anymore roads like the one we were on. My wingman was sitting next to me with his earbuds in, watching some show that he had downloaded onto his phone. So not to disturb him, I slid the visor down on the truck and just kept rolling into the sunset.

Darkness slowly started creeping in, and our destination seemed much farther than I expected, but with a half tank of diesel and full can of Dr. Pepper, I kept going until the sun finally made its last descent for the night.

Around 10 pm, I finally had enough driving for the day and was ready to find somewhere to sleep for the night. It had been a long day and driving in a place that I have never been before, was very tiring. We had stopped at several places along the route to see if there were any vacancies, but most of the places were booked because of all the tourist in town for summer vacation.

A little after midnight I was tired of driving. I didn't care where we ended up, I just needed some sleep and needed it fast. We exited mile marker 90, and went to the Walmart there in town, so that I could park in the parking lot to get me some rest. That little town was called Rifle, Colorado. And I thought to myself, what a kind of name is *Rifle* for a town. Too bad they did not name the town *Daisy*.

# CHAPTER SIX

## *Highway Thirteen*

The next morning, we woke up early to the sun rising over the mountains. It was a great feeling watching the sun rise coming up from behind the mountains. The view was different from what we were used to in Texas. After a few minutes, my son was starting to move around, and I knew he would be hungry soon, because what 15-year-old boy is never hungry?

We stopped at the McDonalds there in town so that we could sit down and relax for a few minutes before getting back on the road. And I knew this would be our last meal in a restaurant before we got to our campsite. I ordered an extra cup of coffee for the road because I knew I would need it for the drive, because our next stop would be our campsite.

After breakfast we were back on the road, headed North on Colorado State Highway 13, and our adventures were about to begin.

I looked at my phone to see how many miles Meeker was from Rifle in case my son or I needed to make a restroom stop on the way. State Highway 13 was a quiet ride, and there were hardly any cars on the road. I did not care because I was so excited to finally get a chance to spend some time with my son for his birthday.

The drive towards Meeker was very peaceful. We started to see deer grazing in the distant every few miles. It was a completely different scenery from what I was used to in Texas. My son had finished his last episode of whatever show he was watching and was looking around at the mountains asking me are we there yet. "Almost, not much farther to go." I said, as we pulled into the first gas station I saw. "Let's run inside really quick and use their restrooms and if you need anything, let's get it now." Before leaving the gas station, I decided on another large cup of coffee, because this would probably be my last cup, and I did not want to pass on the opportunity.

We had about an hour and twenty minutes left on our drive before we would finally arrive to our destination at Browns park. I had already called to make sure they had campsites available, and the man on the phone reassured me that there would be plenty left to choose from.

It was a little before noon before we finally pulled off the dusty road into the campgrounds, and I could tell that we wouldn't have a problem finding a good campsite, because the place looked like a ghost town. After talking with the man in the office, he gave us any choice of where we wanted to be, and explained to us the process for paying for our campsite as well as all of the rules that we had to abide by while we were there.

My son and I drove to the end of the campgrounds before deciding on which one would be the best location for us to set up our tents and unload the truck. We chose the very last one on the left. It had the most shade at that time, and I did not want to spend the week camping in the sun.

I could tell that he was excited to finally be here, he kept staring at the pretty Green water, asking me if we could go fishing. I said, "After we get the truck unloaded, and our tent set up, we can go." I could not wait either, because two days on the road, has been exhausting and I was ready for some fresh air and relaxation. Within about forty minutes, we had the truck unloaded, tent set up, and our poles in hand and headed down to the Green River to see what fishing was really like in Colorado.

Over the past few weeks, I had been reading about all the different types of fish in this area, and I was ready to try and catch something else besides catfish. I wanted to catch one of those monster trouts that I have been reading so much about on the internet. We spent around two hours wading in the water, casting our lines out and looking for the perfect spot that would get the most action. The water was only about three to four feet deep in most places, but it was beautiful, and I was enjoying the view more than anything else.

I had bought my son about 10 different lures, and within the two hours we were there, he must have tried four different lures and was not having any luck at all. I said, "Son, let's go and check out the waterfall, and we can come back this evening to see if we get lucky."

Our campsite was about a 10-minute walk from where we were in the water. I wanted to get to the waterfall and see if I could find anything before it got too late. Around three o'clock, we turned into Vermillion Waterfall, off State Highway 318. There was no one there, but the waterfall was beautiful. It must have been a thirty-foot drop to the bottom, and the water was rushing very fast, for such a small place. My son wanted to go to the top of the waterfall so that he could see if any fish were swimming through the water.

While we were up there, I decided I would take a few minutes to sit down and relax, and just take in the view, plus I wanted to try out my new binoculars as well. After a few minutes, my son came and sat next to me, and asked me what I was doing, and I told him that I was looking for something in the field that did not belong. We must have sat up there for about thirty minutes to an hour, taking turns, looking through my new binoculars. Suddenly, my son screams, "Dad I found something!" He handed me the binoculars and told me to look on the right side, at the top of the hill. After a few seconds, I finally saw what it was that he was talking about. There stood an aluminum t-post, like the kind you would find along a barb wire fence.

There it was, sitting in the middle of the field with nothing else around. No other post was close by, no barb wire laying on the ground, just a lonely aluminum post sitting in the middle of the field. My son and I were super excited, we found the blaze that everyone had been searching for and it was right there in front of our faces.

We made our way down from the waterfall, to get a closer look at the aluminum post. And as we walked up to the post, I started questioning myself, as to why this post had been sitting here in this field untouched and unnoticed.

"Dad, do you think this is where the treasure is buried?" My son said to me, with a huge smile on his face.

"I don't know, but we are about to find out! Go grab the shovel from the truck, while I look around."

Within a few minutes, my son was back with a new shovel we picked up on the way here, and two cold bottles of water. I was getting a little nervous because this was starting to feel like a dream come true. This was the answer to my prayers.

I decided to let my son start digging first because he was younger and in much better shape than me. So hopefully the treasure chest was not buried too deep in the ground, and I could save my energy for counting the gold. After about ten minutes, I could see my son starting to slow down. Plus, we were directly in the sun in the middle of July, and I personally was sweating just standing there.

"Alright my turn. Give me a few swings at it."

I must have dug for another fifteen minutes or so, but in a slower pace than him. And after about thirty minutes, we both had polished off our water bottles and was still dying of thirst. We were starting to get tired from the heat and must have dug down about two feet at that point before I told my son, lets take a break for a while.

Back at the truck, we must have sucked down 2 full bottles of water each before we even started talking about anything in particular.

"Hey David, what do you think?"

"I don't know, but we are pretty deep already." My son said.

"Let's head back to the campsite and do a little more fishing before it gets dark. And in the morning before it gets too hot, we will come back and search some more."

Back at the campsite, we made a quick snack before heading to the river. But where our campsite was located, we could see the water flowing fast in some places. I could tell that he was looking at the same thing as me. It didn't take my son long to finish his sandwich and chips before he had his pole in his hand and was ready to go.

"Ok, give me a few minutes, and I'll walk down there with you."

The water was flowing pretty fast towards the outside of the river, and that was the spot that I wanted to try fishing from so that the current would take my lure further downstream. And give me a better chance at snatching up one of those monster trouts. We must have been in the water for about an hour when all of a sudden, I felt something jerking on my pole. And lucky for me, I had my drag set right because that fish hit that lure so hard, it started running with the current.

"David, look! I got something!" I yelled as he was walking towards me. "Get your line out of the way, this is the one." After a few minutes of going back and forth with the fish, I finally wore him out before bringing him in to shore. I was so excited to finally have caught something, especially being our first day out in the water.

It was starting to get dark, and we decided to head back to the campsite with our dinner. The sun was already starting to set, and I told my son that we should save the fish for another night because I was starting to get tired from the long drive.

The next morning, when I woke up, the sun was starting to make its way up in the eastern sky. I could not believe how beautiful Colorado was. I was ready to get back to the waterfall but decided to take some time and read through the book again before heading back to the aluminum marker.

About twenty minutes into reading *My War For Me*, I could hear my son starting to move around in the tent. And he wasn't going to move any faster unless he smelt something to eat. The coals were still hot from the night before, and we had plenty of firewood in the back of the truck, so I decide to grab a few small sticks to cook breakfast over. For breakfast we had a few eggs that we had already boiled at the house, and some sausage patties that I wanted to cook in the cast iron skillet. And of course, the moment he smelt sausage cooking, he was wide awake.

It was around 7:30 a.m., when we were packed and headed back to the waterfall. On the way in, I noticed one of the aluminum posts on the road at mile marker eighteen, had a faded pink ribbon wrapped around it. Who would put a pink ribbon on an aluminum post in the middle of nowhere? It was definitely in an odd place, but someone must have put it there for a reason.

The waterfall was just another two miles down the road, and I was getting more anxious by the minute wondering if we were about to be millionaires. I couldn't wait to open up the chest and see all the gold coins that I had read about in the book.

As we turned onto the bumpy road, leading up to the waterfall, I didn't see anyone around, or any cars parked in the area. What a relief it was to not have to worry if someone walked up on us while we were searching for the treasure. We decided that we would back the truck down the trail to the waterfall so that when we find the treasure chest, we wouldn't have far to walk. Plus, after yesterday, I wanted to have the ice chest closer to us in case we ran out of water again.

"Dad, do you think that the treasure is really there?"

"Son, I really hope it is."

By this time, we were already parked and walking down to the post, which was only a 100' or more from the truck. This time, I decided that I would go down into the hole first to show my son how its supposed to be done. It didn't take me but ten minutes before I had to tap out and change places with him.

The sun was starting to warm up the sky and I could tell that he was getting tired himself. By this time, we must have been about four-foot-deep, and still no sign of any treasure. My son wanted to go take a swim in the waterfall, but I wasn't ready to walk away just yet. So, I told him to go ahead, and that I would be over there in a few minutes.

I sat there on the edge of the hole trying to figure out how an eighty-year-old man would have dug deeper than me and my son combined. Looking down into the hole, it appeared that we were close to four foot deep, if not farther. By this point, I was starting to get discouraged, so I decided that I would head over to the waterfall, to see what my son was doing, and to leave that hole for another day.

That evening me and my son decided to get back into the water to see if we could catch a few more trout, for dinner that night. I had packed a few sides that was easy to cook if we had gotten lucky and caught some fish. And I was hoping that our luck would get a little better than the treasure hunt was going.

The river water looked much greener than before, and it was also flowing a lot slower but that shouldn't stop us from finding a good spot to fish. We pretty much had the entire area to ourselves. Every now and then, we would see a group of rafters coming down the river from Utah, but they didn't seem to stick around long before being picked up and driven away. Either way, this is what I've been needing, peace and quiet.

The next morning after we ate breakfast and cleaned up a little bit, we decided that we would give it one last try at the waterfall. We had already come too far to walk away empty handed.

It was around 8:00 a.m., when we pulled into the waterfall, and to my surprise we saw someone down at the bottom of the waterfall taking pictures. He was a younger male in his mid-twenties, with long thin blue pants on, and an old t-shirt on. He looked like maybe he was just starting out his career as a photographer or possibly just got a new camera as a gift. But I was curious as to what he was really doing at the waterfall so early in the morning. After we parked the truck, we decided we would walk down there and further investigate him before we got back started on our treasure hunt.

"Good morning!" He said, as we walked up.

"Good morning." I responded as I observed him standing on one of the bigger boulders by the water. I noticed that he had an older radio sitting on a blanket playing some music that I had never heard before. "What is that playing on your radio?"

He responded, "That is something my grandmother would listen to on the radio, *Comin' in On a Wing & A Prayer.*"

There was something about that song that I had recognized but was not quite sure from where. I figured it would be a good idea to walk over and introduce myself.

"I am Reed, and this is my son, David."

"Oh yes, I am Bill, short for William. So, do you guys come out here often?"

"No, we are from Texas, but we came out here to spend some father and son time together. And came to check out the fishing spots in the area." I said while staring up at the waterfall. "What about you?"

"I live a few miles away, and I come to the waterfall every so often to take a few photos and watch the sunrise."

After I realized that he wasn't another treasure hunter, I decided that it was safe to say goodbye and wait for him to leave.

"William, it was nice meeting you, we are going to go walk around and check out the area." I said to him as we waved goodbye.

"It was nice meeting ya'll too." He responded.

After saying goodbye to William at the waterfall, we headed back up the hill, to the truck to gather a few supplies while we waited on him to leave the area.

My son asked, "Dad do you think he is looking for the treasure?"

"It doesn't look like it, but we will wait and see what he does."

A few minutes later, we saw William walking towards the main road to the street. And I thought to myself how odd it was that he didn't even have a car, and maybe he lives some where close by, within walking distance. After William disappeared onto the road, me and my son grabbed a few things from the truck and headed down to our spot. While walking up, I kept thinking to myself, how great it would be to find the treasure. And that some of my problems at home, would soon get better.

This time, I decided I would get down into the hole first so that I could probe the ground with the shovel and all of the walls around me. Still nothing, but a few rocks in the dirt that sounded like a chest when I hit the shovel in the ground. By this time, I was already sweating through my shirt and needed some water. I grabbed my son's hand so that he could pull me out of the hole, and then I lowered him down so that he could clean up my mess.

We gave it another twenty minutes of digging, when I finally came to the conclusion that an eighty-year-old man could not have dug this deep alone.

"David, come on out. There's nothing here, let's take a break and we can come back to this later this evening."

"Yeah, because I don't feel anything with my shovel."

After pulling my son out of the hole, we took a few minutes to suck down as much water as possible, while I thought about what plan B would be.

"Come on, lets go for a walk, and check out the area." I said as I lifted myself off the ground. "Let's take a look on the other side of the creek and see what's over there. You never know what we will see."

# CHAPTER SEVEN

## *Lonely Thoughts*

It was the middle of January and so much had occurred in my life since my trip to the waterfall with my son. My home life had changed completely, and I didn't have much to look forward to at that time. I was sort of dropping into a state of depression.

There wasn't a lot on the TV that night, and while I was scrolling through channels, I noticed my TTOTC book, sitting on the shelf next to the TV. I hadn't opened that book up in over five months, because I had been preoccupied with the new norm in my life.

What the hell, I thought! There's nobody here, and really nothing on TV, why not take a chance and see if my luck was ready to change. I pulled the book from the shelf to examine it, as if it were my first time to have ever held that book. It looked brand new as if there was something different about the book that I hadn't noticed before. That night, I decided that I would take some time and re-read through the book and try to understand what the author was really trying to say.

As the night grew late, I noticed several things about the book that I hadn't noticed before. Some of the chapters in the book only had one or two pages in them, while *My War For Me*, must have had over 20 something pages. And the other thing that I noticed; in all the times he mentions the word Million. Which was very similar to the name of the waterfall that I searched.

There was so much information in his book, that I didn't quite know where to start. At that point in my life, I was ready for something to change. I was ready for an adventure.

After about a week or so, I decided that it was time to get up off the couch and do somethings for myself. And since I had never seen snow, or snow on top of the mountains, I figured that this would be the perfect opportunity to have an adventure of a lifetime.

It was a good thing that I had saved my credit card points because I had been waiting for something big, and this was the perfect opportunity to capitalize on those points. After learning how to book a plane ticket with my points and setting up an account with a rental car company, I was all set to plan my trip. The only thing I was lacking was setting a date.

I believe it was around January 20th, when I decided to act. I wasn't getting any younger, and my life of just sitting on the couch was starting to get pretty lame. After a long conversation with my wife, and telling her my plans, I was ready to take the next step. The next day without any hesitation, I was on a plane headed to Colorado. I had everything set up as far as my rental was concerned, and I figured I would just wing it with the hotels along the way. This way, I am not tied to a schedule for most of my trip.

Landing in Colorado and seeing snow for the first time was awesome, this was my first time ever seeing something so amazing. I was super excited to be off my couch and doing the one thing that I enjoyed the most, and that is the outdoors. After getting my luggage, I headed outside of the terminal and made my way to island #4, to wait for the shuttle to transport me to the rental car company.

Denver was not all that I thought it would be, it was somewhat similar to Dallas, but the moment I drove out of the city limits, everything changed. The scenery was so beautiful, mountains as high up as I could see, covered with snow all the way down. Even the lakes were frozen solid, and people were skiing on them, having the best time ever.

As I traveled down I-70, I passed through a little town called Vail. What a coincidence that Fenn mentioned Vale in his memoir. I didn't pay much attention to that before, or maybe it was just me over thinking things again. A little while later, after passing through Gypsum before getting to Rifle, I started re-thinking my first thoughts. Maybe the book is really a road map, and all the towns will guide me to the treasure.

It didn't take but a few hours, and I was entering the town of Craig, Colorado, when I decided that I would go ahead and find me some where nice to stay for the night. Plus, I was starting to get a little hungry from traveling all day. I had found a little travel lodge located on the main drag, that still had a few vacancies left, and the rooms were cheap for what I was expecting.

My little room was cozy, it had central heat, carpet throughout, including the bathroom, but most importantly it had clean sheets. Now all I needed was a hot meal and a stiff drink, to finish off my night, before heading to bed.

The next morning when I woke up to go start the truck, I noticed that the food I had bought the day before was frozen solid, including my bananas and water. What a great way to start off my adventure, with frozen food. Around 6:00 a.m., I had everything packed up and was ready to go find me some coffee, before heading over to the waterfall. I wanted to get there early, because this trip, was not all about pleasure. It was a business trip, and I was here to bring home a treasure chest for my family.

On my way to the waterfall, I spotted two baby deer's standing on the side of the road. They looked confused, on exactly which direction they wanted to go, but either way, I decided it was best to slow down, in case they chose the same direction that I was headed. From town, the waterfall was about 100 plus miles away, and this gave me some time to think as I made my way towards, MayBELL, Colorado.

MayBELL, looked like it would become the next ghost town of Colorado. There was only one store in town, and the rest of the commercial places looked like they haven't been open in a while. I don't even recall the town having a stop sign, that's how small it was.

About midway through town, I recognize my street that takes me into the park. And that road is just as lonely and isolated as the little town I passed through. The waterfall was about forty miles away, from town, so I knew to leave myself enough fuel, to get back to town, in case my rental truck starts getting low on gas.

A little before 8:00 a.m., I had pulled onto that bumpy road, leading up to the waterfall. And as usual, there was no one there. I was alone, and the only people that knew exactly where I would be located was my family back in Texas. So, I had to plan on being very careful at the waterfall, because the only location to get cell phone service was about thirty miles away.

The sun was starting to warm things up, and the blocks of ice on the ground was beginning to melt. Thank God I rented a truck with four-wheel drive, because I was starting to slip and slide as I drove into the parking area. And the last thing I needed to happen, was getting the truck stuck and be forced to spend hours out there alone.

By this time, I wish I had bought two cups of coffee, because my first cup had gone down pretty smooth, and I usually enjoy having several cups of coffee in the morning. This adventure was not turning out how I had envisioned it would. But that is the city boy in me, not the mountain man that I would soon come to know.

Walking down to the waterfall, I noticed that the aluminum marker was still sitting in the same spot, that I had found it several months ago. The area looked so much different than it did in the summertime. In certain areas, I saw snow slowly melting on the ground, and ice was falling down from the waterfall. On my drive in, my truck was registering the temperature to be 10 degrees outside, but with the sun shining down on me, it felt somewhere in the range of 20 degrees.

I wanted to start my search looking down, as the poem states, so I figured I would start looking about 20 feet from the post, and make my way in a circle, so that I would cover all of the areas around the marker and didn't miss anything. Within about an hour or so, I needed to get back to the truck so that I could try and warm up, because the Colorado cold air, was nothing to play around with. And I didn't want to chance catching a cold or the flu in this weather.

Thirty minutes had passed by pretty fast, and I could feel my feet starting to warm up again. I knew that I couldn't stay in the truck all day, I needed to get back out there into the cold and go find this treasure. But this time, I brought my binoculars, so that I could look a little bit closer at everything before deciding what my next course of action would be.

Even with the cold air, I still packed a few water bottles just in case I got thirsty walking around looking for more clues. On the way down the dirt road to the waterfall, I pulled out my binoculars, to get a better view of the area, and see if there was something that I had missed before. Around the creek area, I noticed several branches on the trees had been broken. Some of the branches look about as thick as my wrist. Whatever animal that had done that, must have been a monster, and I sure hope that I don't run into it while searching for clues.

After giving it a few more minutes of not finding anything around the post, I made my way over to the creek to see if I could find any animal tracks or if I could see what animals live in the area. The only tracks that I had found was a few deer tracks and a lot of rabbit droppings everywhere. Along the creek, I noticed a few more trees with different breaks in them, many of them were different sizes, and some were down low, and others were up high. There must have been five or six trees along the creek, that I noticed, all having broken limbs. Could an animal really have done this? If so, why did they only leave the limbs hanging, and not pull them off completely?

I had so many questions about what I was seeing, so I decided that I would start keeping notes of everything that I had found, and taking pictures was the best way to keep track of my adventure. The very first tree that I had walked up to, I noticed that there were two breaks, one on each side of the tree.

Not long after snapping a photo of the broken tree limb, my fingers went numb. I tried warming them back up, even putting my gloves back on, and that didn't seem to help. Even tried blowing hot air on them, to see if that would help the pain, but it didn't help either. Eventually I noticed that most of my fingers were starting to turn purple and the pain was getting to be unforgiving.

As I sat there crying, because of the pain, I knew something strange had happened, but did not know exactly what had happened to me at that time. Within about twenty or thirty minutes, I slowly started regaining feeling again in my hands. I must have had a guardian angel watching over me, because there was no way in hell, that I should have survived that trip.

# CHAPTER EIGHT

## Stone Marker

I have always lived my life making deals and paying those debts back no matter what. Many people who know me, know that if we shook hands on whatever agreement we made, then I would follow through on my end, and expect them to do the same.

Before this adventure even began, things were going great for me in life. My business was doing great, we were in the beginning phases of a new project. I was married to a beautiful wife, had a beautiful home, and my kids were healthy and happy. And on top of everything, I had plenty of money in the account, and was only a few years away from being debt free.

After my return from my first trip in 2019, things in my life took a turn. My world was flipped upside down, and everything that I once knew or loved, was in jeopardy of being lost. Over those next few months, while fighting to save my marriage and business, I received a lot of calls from a number that I didn't recognize. Then one day, I noticed several missed calls from the same number.

When the next call came in, I answered it on the second ring. It was a voice on the phone from a man that I could not understand. The only thing that I somewhat understood was vera cruz. After the call had ended, I remembered sitting there on my couch, trying to piece together the entire phone conversation, and that is when I noticed my book sitting on the shelf. But this time, it was laying there opened to page 83.

That night, while sitting on my couch, reading through TTOTC, I noticed something that I did not notice before. The author had a time stamp in the book, standard time as well as military time. Why would he do that? I kept asking myself several times. After skimming through the remainder of the book, I realized it was not done anywhere else in the book or was he intentionally marking this time for a reason.

On March 13th, 2020, I decided it was time to go pay another visit to the waterfall. Maybe this trip, I would find a few more clues needed to get me closer to Fenn's treasure chest.

The next day, I booked a flight with United Airlines and lucky for me, the flights were still cheap because most of the states were still on lock down, but as long as the planes were still flying, I was ready.

As the day went by, I grew more and more excited about my trip. This treasure hunt adventure was giving my mind something else to think about besides my family. Twenty hours left until my plane takes off, but there were still quite a few things that I needed to do before I left. One of the things on my list to do was grocery shopping. The kids had eaten almost everything up while they were home from school, so I figured while I am out looking for some winter socks, I could grab them a few meals to last them for a few days.

At Walmart, most everyone was walking around with mask on there faces, people were keeping their distances, while they were going through the aisles. One family even had a mask on their baby. Why would anyone bring a child to the grocery store to only have them wear a mask? Things were changing in the world, and they were changing fast.

After about an hour into my shopping fiasco, I was beyond ready to get to the mountains and not have to see anyone. Finally, I made it to the checkout aisle, and there stood these two old ladies, neither one had a mask on. I was surprised because the way our government was describing this virus, the old people did not have a chance. Neither one of the two ladies even seemed like they were worried about the virus. They were standing there in the checkout aisle, whispering and chuckling with each other as if they were teenagers.

That night while packing my bag, I was going through some old pictures from when me and my son first went on our trip. In every picture, you could see how happy he was to be in the mountains, and for me, I was happy too.

This trip somehow felt different, some type of way, it almost feels as though something had been calling me back to that place. The day was finally here, it was March 15th, 2020 and my plane was scheduled to take off in a few hours. I had packed just enough to get me through the next few days.

After arriving at the airport, I found myself standing on the same island waiting for my shuttle to bring me to my rental car. During my drive, I started to notice somethings that I didn't notice before. There was so many road markers or places that was referenced in the book. Even going through the different towns, they all seemed to somehow have been referenced in the book.

This time, I decided that I would take a different route to the waterfall. So instead of driving all the way to Rifle, I decided that I would take State Highway 9 North towards Kremmling. Hopefully, this route is a little more scenic than my previous route, and possible cut my drive time down by a few minutes. Plus, I had heard about a great place on SH 9, that a few friends from work were talking about. I believe it was Middle Park Meat Co., and since I had missed breakfast, I was ready for a hot meal.

I had made it to the waterfall about two hours before sunset and was a little worried that the aluminum marker would have been removed. To my surprise, it was still sitting right there, untouched and unnoticed. The area was still empty, and no one was around, I decided to go sit on top of the waterfall and relax for a minute.

As I sat there by the edge of the waterfall, throwing rocks over, I saw something from a distance moving around in the bushes about 500' out. I pulled my Minox binoculars from my bag to see if I could get a better view through them.

Looking through my binoculars, I spotted a rabbit moving around at the bottom of the valley. It was underneath a bush I assume getting ready for the night. As I sat there looking around to see if anything else was down there, I saw someone sitting between the high grass in the water. It was a little girl playing in the creek, she looked around twelve or thirteen years old.

When I pulled my binoculars down, she had disappeared. I started looking all around that area to see if I could see her, but nobody was there. I knew for a fact that I had seen her, but where did she go?

Something strange was going on, and I needed answers. I needed to know what happened to that little girl. After a few more minutes, I decided that I would try looking through my binoculars again. Hoping to find her somewhere, and there she was, standing still in the middle of the creek. And only this time, she was not playing in the water, she was staring at me and pointing with her left hand. Slowly I moved my binoculars into the direction that she was pointing, but all I could see was the marker in the middle of the field. The same marker that I found on my first visit to the waterfall.

As I started to move my binoculars back towards the little girl, I spotted someone walking in the shadows. It was William, the young man that I had met during the summer, taking photos of the waterfall. As he moved closer to marker, I noticed he was holding his camera and taking photos of the little girl standing in the water. What were they doing? Why are they in the middle of this field taking photos?

After a few minutes of watching them, I lowered my binoculars to get a better view on them both, and then again, they were gone. Something strange was happening, and I couldn't say a word to anyone because no one would ever believe this.

As I made my way off the top of the waterfall, I noticed that the temperature had started dropping quite a bit, and the sun was beginning to set.

But first I needed to go see what William was photographing. Because something inside of me needed to know. While standing there at the marker looking into the sunset, I finally saw what William was looking at. And it was the most amazing view that I had ever seen.

Back at the hotel, as I laid there in the bed, trying to wrap my brain around what I had seen. Trying to figure out where that little girl came from and what was she doing? I had so many questions that I couldn't answer, but it was killing me to find out Forrest Fenn's Secret.

The next morning, I woke up early and started me a pot of coffee in the room while I brushed my teeth and packed my bag. I knew I had a long day because my flight home was scheduled to leave around 7pm. And I couldn't risk missing another flight, because I had to be back at work early the next morning. After my coffee was done brewing, I filled up my thermos and made me a cup for the road. It was around 6 am, and I was out the door.

On my drive back to the waterfall, I drove past a sign that I had never seen before. It was a horseshoe sign, marking the entrance for a ranch that is located off the road. Is it strange that I had driven past it several times before, but never noticed it until today?

After about an hour and half drive, I finally made it back to the waterfall around 7:30 a.m. And for some reason, this area didn't have any snow anywhere, but the temperature was still below freezing. I wanted to try and see if I could find that little girl again, so I made my way back up to the top of the waterfall to the same spot I was sitting at the night before. The field was still empty, except for a couple of deer grazing towards the edge of the creek.

While sitting on top of the waterfall, I spotted a mysterious glow in the water. Something was there, but I couldn't make out exactly what it was. As I approached the water, I could see something moving in the middle of the creek. I don't really remember what happened next but for some reason, I felt my arm being pulled down into that icy cold water. I could feel the needles sticking me in my arm. But whatever it was, kept pulling me down, to the point that my body was eventually underwater.

After a few seconds, I could feel someone grabbing my hand, and pulling me down farther into the creek. When I opened up my eyes, the little girl was right there in front of me. Looking me dead in the eyes, and I could feel her telling me that everything would be okay.

What was it that she was trying to show me? She held my hand on a huge stone and held my hand in place with both of her hands. I could slowly feel my body becoming numb in the icy cold water. As my body started to relax, the little girl leaned over towards me, and whispered into my ear,

"Hold on, don't let go."

# CHAPTER NINE

## Valley of Death

Over the next few weeks, my mind continued to run. I could not figure out how I survived being in that ice-cold water. Neither do I remember how long I was down there. But I knew someone was watching over me and kept me alive down there. So many questions that I kept asking myself but did not have the answers too.

On the Saturday before Easter, while in a dead sleep, I could feel something pulling at my hand to wake up. After a while, the tugging continued to grow stronger. And as I started to open my eyes, I remembered seeing a flash of light moving quickly away from me.

Who was it pulling my hand? When I finally opened my eyes, there was nobody there. There was no one else in the room, I was alone and wide awake. Something inside of me was telling me to go see, go back to the waterfall, and see what is really there.

Within a few minutes, I had a flight booked and my bags packed. My flight was scheduled to leave around 7 am. But I had just enough time to write a note to my wife, if for some reason, this was my last and final trip.

I pulled into the waterfall a little bit before 6 pm, and as usual the place was empty, not a soul in sight. So instead of walking to the top of the waterfall, I decided that I would head down towards the marker to find out what I didn't see. But something was different by the marker. I could see a fresh set of footprints in the sand.

I knew it was not my prints, because I always wore the same boots to the waterfall. These prints looked almost like a pair of military boots, and they were an inch or so smaller than mine. After a few minutes at 17:55 (5:55 pm) I could feel the sun shining directly on to my face. The sun was the brightest that I had ever seen, and it was shining directly at me. It was so bright, that I had to put my hands over my eyes just to enjoy the view.

Is this what I was called back to the waterfall to see? Is this really the blaze that everyone has been searching for the past 10 years? This is by far the greatest moment in my life. I have finally found *The Magical Blaze.*

There I was, standing at the aluminum marker, at 5:55 pm looking west at 250 degrees, staring into the sun, as if it were my first time ever to witness something so amazing. I could not believe how magical it really was, and the feeling that came over me, knowing that I was the one searcher to find *The Magical Blaze.*

I stood there for several more minutes watching the sun drop down behind the mountains. I did notice that during its descent, the sun stayed directly over the largest tree in the middle of the valley.

After witnessing the sunset, I headed back to the vehicle to grab me a bite to eat and something to drink. The entire time I was sitting in my vehicle thinking about what I had just witnessed. I also kept thinking about the little girl as well.

It was 7:30 pm when I woke up, and the sky was showing a little bit of daylight left in the day. I decided with what little bit of time that was left, I needed to make my way towards the top of the waterfall before it had gotten any later. While sitting at my little spot on the waterfall, I pulled the binoculars out of my bag so that I could check the area one more time to see if I could find the little girl.

After about ten minutes of looking through my lens, I could see something out in the distance, on the other side of the creek. It looked like two people standing in the shadows by that tree. I really could not see their faces, but I did see that they were standing very close to each other underneath the tree.

As I worked my way down into the valley, I noticed that the water was flowing faster than normal, and I could see where the animals had tried making their way across the water. I spotted several prints on each side in the mud, and it was obvious that this is where they were crossing. I had brought my shovel with me in case I needed it, and this time I did. I used it as a brace to help me cross the fast-moving current to the other side.

Once on the other side of the creek, I started walking through the tall grass towards that tree where I had seen the two figures standing. The grass and brush were about waist high, but I could see a path on the ground, and this was not a man-made trail. As I continued walking along the path, I noticed a very strong smell of pinyon trees and sage brush and could hear small birds chirping through the bushes. Then suddenly, I came to an opening, and could see about six or seven trees grouped together in various places. The brush was no longer present, it was mostly a sandy area, with a few branches on the ground that had fallen over the years.

As I got closer to the tree, I didn't see anyone, or anything that resembled what I saw through my binoculars, not even a footprint in the sand.

Strangely enough, I knew I was not alone. But what was it that I saw through my binoculars? As the sun started to fade behind the mountains, a chill came across my body, I could hear footsteps behind me, as I stood there next to that tree, I heard a voice whispering into my ear, "Look Down."

Shortly before midnight, I was awakened by the sounds of the wind howling through the cracked windows of my jeep. The wind had become so strong as if it were trying to pry the doors open. Looking out the window, I could see the limbs on the trees whipping around in the wind, as though they were calling me to get out and come see. For the next few minutes as I sat there in the Jeep, trying to figure out what was going on, I started to pray to God, asking Him to protect me through this storm. Fear came across my body and I became afraid of what I was seeing in front of me. I couldn't tell if I was dreaming, or if I was really seeing ghost hovering over my vehicle. As scared as I was, I locked the doors and prepared myself for what was about to happen next.  After a few more minutes, the wind started to die down and eventually everything became calm again.  As I sat there alone in the Jeep, listening to small rocks falling from the cliffs above me, wondering was this even real, or if I have crossed the vale.

Something happened that night, that I cannot explain, but whatever it was, was finally gone.  And I was alone with my thoughts, trying to recall how I ended up in the passenger side of the vehicle.  The last thing I remembered was a voice in my ear, telling me to look down. But where?

# CHAPTER TEN

## *Easter Sunday*

The next morning as the sun came up, I grabbed my hiking bag, and headed up to the top of the mountain, so that I could watch the magnificent Colorado sunrise. I made sure to pack me plenty of water, not knowing how long it would be before making it back to the Jeep that day.

As I hiked up to the highest point, I found me a small tree located a few feet from the trail. I figured that this would be the perfect spot to sit and watch the sun come up while enjoying my Vienna sausage and bottle of water.

Within a few minutes, the sun started making its way from behind the mountains towards the east. I had never seen anything so incredible, everything about that sunrise was perfect. This was one of those magical moments that I wish I could have shared with my beautiful wife. Hands down, this is starting off to be the best Easter Sunday ever. While sitting up there watching the sunrise, I took some time to thank God for all that He has done throughout my journeys into the mountains.

After finishing up my breakfast, I started hearing movement a few feet away. Slowly a baby deer poked his head from behind the bush right by the trail where I was sitting. As I sat there watching her walk past me, a few seconds later, more of them started walking by, one after another. There must have been about 15 or 20 of them walking right past me as if I didn't exist. I could tell that they were on a mission, and whatever that mission was, I was pretty sure I wasn't invited. But after the last deer walked by, I waited a few minutes before moving from underneath the tree, because I didn't want to startle them or take a chance of one of them attacking me.

As I began walking back to my parking spot next to the waterfall, a wolf walked out in front of me, and stopped a few feet away from where I was standing. There was no way I was going to run, because I knew with all my training, that the moment I turn my back on that beast, it was over. With only my walking stick handy, I took a deep breath, and stood there staring him in the eyes. Waiting to see if he was going to attack, and if he was, then I needed to be ready to fight back. We both were standing still, waiting for the other to make the first move. Whatever was going to happen next, I was prepared to fight this beast to the very end.

After what seemed like a few minutes, he must have realized that I wasn't backing down from him, or he decided that he was better off finding something smaller to eat. Eventually the wolf vanished into the brush, without making a sound.

Back at the waterfall, the deer were grazing in the tall grass, and some of the smaller deer were nipping at each other's tails. In the herd, it was clear who the alpha deer was, and it was very obvious as to which ones were the elders of pack. Slowly the Alpha deer made its way through the valley as the others followed, and eventually they had all disappeared into the tall grass without making a noise.

The temperature outside was starting to drop, and I knew it was time for me to make my way back across the creek to the tallest tree in the valley. From a distance, something seemed different about the area, as though someone had already been there.

It was around 9 o'clock, when I emptied the trash from my hiking bag, and grabbed a few more bottles of water, so that I could head back over to canvass the area for more clues. On my way down into the valley, I noticed a trail of rabbit droppings and started thinking to myself, seasoned in the soil and started laughing at Fenn's crazy sense of humor.

The water was higher than normal, and my usual path across seemed to be flooded over. I could just try and jump across, but there was no guarantee that I would make it over without falling in. It was probably in my best interest to find another way across, maybe something a little further down creek.

As I reached into my bag to get me a bottle of water, I felt someone's hand touch my left shoulder. Startled I turned around, to find the little girl standing there next to me. Her eyes were fixed onto mine, and I could feel her telling me something. And at that moment, everything went quiet. No more sounds of the rushing water in the creek, or the winds blowing through the trees. Just complete silence, as we looked into each other's eyes.

I could feel my left hand being squeezed, as I looked down, she was standing there next to me, only this time her hair was wet. She was still holding my hand, when she started leading me down towards the creek, and the path that I usually took going across, was now visible. As she led me across the creek, I noticed that the water was flowing at a much slower pace, and the sounds of the waterfall, was slowly starting to fade back in. The usual noises from before was starting to rush back into my ears.

On the other side of the creek, the little girl cupped her right hand around her mouth, and with her left hand, she pulled me in closer so that she could whisper into my ear. She said, "Thank you!" I did not know what for, but I certainly was not going to ask.

The little girl turned around and slowly started walking back into the water, towards the middle of the creek. And just like that, she was gone, and all I could think about, was how tragic her final seconds of life were.

As I started walking towards the tree, I could hear voices blowing in the wind, almost like whispers in my ear. Someone was over there because I could see something moving in the shadows.

As I began to get closer, I noticed something different about the area, things have been moved. There seemed to be more limbs on the ground in random places as if someone or something had shaken the trees, searching for something. Someone was trying to tell me something, but what is it? What are they saying?

I noticed at the center of the tree, there seemed to be branches piled higher than before as if someone was trying to hide something. What was hiding in that tree that I could not see?

And then before I knew it, I was pulling branches over my head, and throwing them behind me. Some were tangled up in other branches and others came out easily. I must have spent about thirty minutes or so, removing years' worth of dead limbs before getting hot and needing a break. The sun was starting to warm things up around me, and I could feel myself starting to sweat, even though it was eighteen degrees outside, I was still getting hot.

A few feet away from where I was working, was a log sitting on the ground, and it was bent at the nose of the tree and looked like a perfect place to take a break.

While sitting there on the log, I could feel something walking up behind me. Looking back, I didn't see anything but a rabbit hiding underneath the brush. It was sitting there just nibbling on the grass, at the bottom of the brush. My heart was still racing a thousand miles an hour, but I was also relieved that it was only a rabbit.

As I turned back around to pick up my water bottle, two women were sitting a few feet away on the sandy ground watching me, with smiles on their faces. "What the...?" I said. Who are these women sitting in front of me? I didn't know what to do, or what to say. There was no running away from this. I wasn't sure if I was dreaming or was this real?

"What are you doing out here? We haven't seen anyone in years walking around here." Said the shorter lady.

"I know that you can hear us, so quit playing possum." Responded the taller of the two.

I stuttered for a moment or two, and finally the words came out of my mouth, "Who are ya'll?"

"We are sisters, our family owns the cemetery across the street from here. We hang out over here during the day, but at night, we head back home to check on things. We're here to help you."

I asked, "Help me with what?" I took another long drink of my water, still trying to figure out what was going on.

"We know what you are looking for, we've been watching you for the past few months. We saw you the very first time you came to the waterfall, we all have been watching you." The taller one said as she stood up and walked over to the tree.

The next morning, when I woke up, I found myself laying in a den on the side of the mountain, looking out at the beautiful waterfall and the group of trees where I had ventured to the day before. What happened to me? How did I find myself so high up here? As I made my way down, I noticed inside the den was rabbit droppings. But no rabbit could have gotten up this high.

Walking back to my Jeep, I could feel the snow touching my face, and the sun was starting to make its way up in the eastern sky. I kept thinking to myself, was it all a dream?

The Jeep was still parked at the bottom of the waterfall and everything seemed to still be there inside of the Jeep. I think it is time for me to head home before something else happens that I cannot explain.

# CHAPTER ELEVEN

## *Directions*

**B**ack home, the kids were excited to see me, or maybe they were just glad I was home to take them out to eat. Still not quite sure which one it was. But I was very glad to finally be home and looking forward to sleeping in my own bed for a change.

After a quick shower and a change of clothes, we were headed out to go find something that was still open. Most of the places were closed, but they were all offering pick up orders or delivery. We all voted on Chinese food since we haven't had it in a while, plus I think the kids were tired of eating burgers and or ramen noodles every night for dinner. I am sure they were ready for something different. Me, I was just ready for a hot meal verses canned sausage and water.

My daughter called in the order while I ran into Walmart to grab me a few things. As I walked around the store for a minute, I started to feel out of place because everyone was wearing masks, or some type of face protection. People were starting to fear the worse, buying up everything on the shelves, standing 6' apart from each other. Things were changing in the world, and by the looks of things, this was becoming the new norm, *Social Distancing.*

Standing in the checkout line, I noticed a whole family wearing face masks, even the kids had masks on. And they were looking at me like I was an alien from another planet. Probably wondering where my mask was. After what I have been through, I didn't think a mask was going to save me, the only One who could help me now, was the Man Upstairs.

As I walked out of the store, I tried showing my receipt to the lady standing at the exit, but she just flagged me on, as if she didn't want me getting close to her. It was a strange feeling, to keep 6' apart from people.

At the Chinese restaurant, my daughter went in to get our food and she had asked me if I had a mask that she could wear inside. And said that it was a requirement when dealing with food workers.

"Look inside the glove box. There should be one in there." I said as I glanced through my phone reading news articles. Before she headed inside, she asked me and my son if we needed anything else before she left.

Sitting there in my truck, I kept thinking about my trip, still trying to put all of the pieces together and thinking about those two ladies that I saw in my dream, wondering was it even a dream. What did she mean, I was not ready? Ready for what?

That night while lying in bed, I messaged my wife to see how she and our son were doing? I didn't tell her much about my trip because she really didn't ask, so I decided to keep the conversation simple. It's been almost a year since she moved out, and everyday has been a struggle for me not having my wife and son at home with me.

We chatted back and forth for a while about her weekend and what all they did for the Easter weekend. My wife sent me a few pictures of our son picking up eggs and putting them into his basket. He looked so happy playing with the *plastic* eggs, I could not believe how big he looked in the pictures. Before we headed to bed, we would always tell each other how much we missed each other, and how we plan to work on our issues together. And as always, I wanted to make sure that my last message for the night said, "I Love You!"

Around 10:30 p.m. is when I started drifting off to sleep, and I could feel my body slowly starting to relax. As I fell deeper into the sleep, I started dreaming about the little girl in the water. Trying to remember where I had seen her before the waterfall. I knew I recognized her face, but from where?

A few minutes later, I woke up almost immediately. I remembered where I saw her at? It was the McDonalds in Stephenville, Texas. She was the little girl standing by the door when we walked in. I remember exactly when we stopped in Stephenville on our way home from Colorado. It was her, the little girl from the waterfall.

These trips were starting to become too much for me to handle. I needed to take a break for a while. I needed to spend some time at home with the kids, they have been a big help to me during my trips to Colorado.

But first, I needed to get some sleep, my shift starts at 4 am and my body was exhausted, but my mind was still spinning in circles about the events surrounding this treasure hunt. The harder I tried sleeping, the more I thought about that little girl, wondering who she was? Why did I see her in that small town, and then again at the waterfall? So many questions were keeping me awake tonight to the point that I was just lying in bed wide awake.

Alexa started going off at her usual time, and I knew that it was too late to call in sick because the only person that would get screwed is my relief, and that's not the type of person that I am.

"Alexa I am awake!"

"Hmmm I don't think so." Alexa responds.

"Alexa five more minutes."

Finally, I had enough of going back and forth with Alexa, so I just got up and left her in the room with the alarm still going. I grabbed my keys and went outside to start the truck and get a few drags in of my cigarette before heading in to start cleaning up for my shift.

I was just thankful that it was a weekend shift, so usually not a lot going on at work, mostly routine task that I've done a million times. This drive to work was somewhat different. As I drove past the cemetery, I started seeing shadows of people standing on the side of the road. Each one was standing still as though they were watching a parade go by.

Now I am starting to get worried, not knowing if this is from a lack of sleep, or am I really seeing something. Whatever it was that I saw, I could not risk turning back around to go investigate because I was already running late for work.

The only people that somewhat listens to me ramble about this treasure hunt are my children and my good friend from work, Derrick Johnson. But they were all getting to the point, that they were starting to get worried about me. My wife, whenever I would bring up my trips or how I am feeling, it only seems to push her further away. But as much as I wanted to abandon this treasure hunt, I couldn't. Something keeps pulling me back in, and I needed to find out the truth, I need to know what Fenn's secret was.

As the next few weeks went by, I tried focusing on cleaning things out of my house, making minor repairs, like changing light bulbs, fixing the garbage disposal and other things that I've neglected the past few months while traveling. The kids were excited about me being home, they were getting bored because school was cancelled for the coronavirus, so they were doing whatever they could to keep me entertained. There weren't many options of things to do, with everything going on in the world, we were limited to watching movies, playing board games, and mainly catching up on sleep.

But for me, as hard as I tried focusing on what's at home, my mind was still being pulled back to the waterfall. There was something in his book that I was missing, and I kept asking myself, why would someone leave a treasure in the mountains for the world to come find? How was it that after 10 years, I was the one to walk straight to the marker that had sat in that valley unnoticed for so long? Out of all the people that have searched for the treasure chest, why haven't I seen any other searchers in the area?

So many questions that I had, wondering why me out of all the other treasure hunters, why me? Over the next few weeks, I kept trying to make sense of the numbers that was in the book. Why was everything 1000 feet, how does anyone know what 1000 feet is while flying in a plane?

Then I remembered the markings on the road markers. He specifically marked them for a reason, but driving 65 mph down a road, there is so much that a person will miss unless they are paying close attention.

"That's it, that's the answer!" as I yelled to myself. Planes don't fly miles per minute, they fly knots. Twelve miles a minute, means mile marker twelve. And from there, each 1000 feet, is really a mile. Now it's starting to make sense. Starting at mile marker twelve, while traveling south two miles towards the storage area. At mile marker 14, at the intersection, the tree on the right is his wingman.

Now I finally see how he is giving directions; I know exactly where to go from there. It was one of the very first places that I had traveled to in the beginning, when I found a guillotine at the dead end. This entire time, he was giving me directions to exactly where I needed to go.

# CHAPTER TWELVE

## Finding the Bells

The day before my flight was scheduled to leave, I was finishing up my graveyard shift. I was starting to get more anxious to get back to the waterfall and test out my theory. Throughout the night, I continued going over the directions in my head, trying to talk myself out of what I read. Something about this trip didn't feel right, but I knew that if I didn't go, I would continue to wonder what if.

The next morning, my daughter woke me up as planned, because I was afraid of missing my flight, and I didn't want to chance me not hearing my alarm clock while I was sleeping. On the way to the airport, we stopped to get a few things from the store for my trip, and a well needed cup of coffee. Traveling on a few hours of sleep was exhausting, but I was hoping to catch a few more hours on the plane.

On the plane, I noticed that there were more travelers flying again than the previous month. People were starting to venture out of their homes again and getting back to the norm. It felt somewhat comforting seeing other faces back in public places. The flight was as usual, the flight attendants gave their usual presentation on where the emergency exits were, how to use the life vest, and what to do in case the plane had to make an emergency landing. And as always, no one paid attention to the presentations.

It was a normal flight into Denver, most everyone stayed in their seats, and the flight attendants didn't come around and offer snacks or drinks as they usually did. But with travel down, and fear of COVID-19, no one really complained. After about 2 hours into the flight, the pilot came across the intercom to announce how many minutes before landing and asked everyone to buckle up and prepare for light turbulence.

I didn't get much sleep on the flight as expected. I was hoping for some sleep, so that I wouldn't be tired during my drive to the waterfall, but with so much on my mind, it was hard to sleep. Around one o'clock, we pulled into our gate, and as soon as the plane stopped rolling, several people jumped up and started grabbing their bags as if they were in a race to exit the plane.

As everyone exited the plane, I noticed a lady putting a mask on her rescue dog, and I thought to myself, what has this world come too? Now animals are wearing mask. This was just too much for me to handle, I needed to get away from people, as far as I possibly could.

Within minutes, I was back standing on that same island, waiting for the shuttle to show up. This was probably the first time that I can remember where

I had to wait on the shuttle. With everyone afraid to travel, it appeared that more than just the restaurants are struggling to find customers.

My shuttle finally arrived to take me to the rental car place, and from there it only takes a few minutes to pick out a vehicle before my journey began. The weather in Denver was beautiful, this was probably the first time in months that I was able drive with the windows down and could feel the sun shining while I drove. I was ready to finally get back to the waterfall so that I can see if the directions from the book were correct.

When I pulled onto SH-318 around 7:30 pm, the sun had already begun to set, and time was running out for me to do any searching tonight. But it was still early enough for me to at least check to see if the directions were accurate before the night was over. During the drive on SH-318, I didn't see one car driving past me, nor was there anyone behind me. The road was lonely, and with no phone service, there was no one to talk to or anything playing on the radio.

I had never seen this sunset before, as if I were driving to a completely different place. This sunset seemed like it was burning into the side of the mountains with the way the light was beaming from the sky. While driving, I decided to snap a few photos of the sunset, so I grabbed my phone that was sitting in the passenger seat and took a couple pictures through the windshield of the SUV. After reviewing my photos, I decided that it was time for a cold Dr. Pepper and my turkey sandwich that I'd pick up from the gas station, a few miles back.

As I continued my descent into the sunset, something made me curious as to which direction I was driving and remembered the compass on my phone was pretty dead on even without service. While driving I started scrolling through my phone looking for the compass app, and noticed that my wife, had sent me a text, wishing me a safe trip and to hurry back home. I must have picked up service for a minute or two while I was driving to get her message.

With my compass open on my phone, it started doing something that I had never seen before. The dial on the compass must have spun around 3 or 4 times until it finally came to a complete stop. After it had quit spinning, I pointed my phone towards the sunset to see exactly which direction I was traveling. It was showing 90 degrees into the sun. And before I even had a chance to do anything else, I spotted a family of deer on the side of the road, and knew that if I didn't slow down, one of them would possibly run into the road and cause me to wreck. Standing off the road about fifty feet, there was two older deer with huge racks on the top of their heads. They were possibly the first two that I had seen all winter, with antlers.

As I passed the waterfall on my left, I started thinking again about my compass and what it said. There was no way I was traveling 90 degrees into the sun. That would mean, that I was traveling east into the sunset, and that is impossible. I quickly reached for my phone again, to double check myself, in case I had misread it, or had something set wrong on my phone. And again, my phone continued telling me, that I was traveling east.

I started thinking in my head and kept repeating to myself that the sun rises in the east and sets in the west. So why is it now, my compass is acting strange? It had worked before when I was standing at the first marker I had found. Why was it not working now?

There were other things for me to worry about than my phone. I needed to focus on why I made this trip back to the mountains, and that was mainly to check the directions that I had found in TTOTC.

On the left was the turn off to the Gate of Ladore campsite, but I needed to keep going a couple more miles until I reached mile marker 12. As I got within 1000 feet of the mile marker, I noticed four trees on the side of the road, and thought to myself, that those were the four switches he turned on and started laughing to myself. How he could have written such a great book, for only one person to understand.

After mile marker twelve, I turned the car around and started my countdown to see if everything added up exactly how the book described it. I drove approximately two miles, and on the right at 30 degrees, I found my wingman sitting right there waiting for me to turn in. As I went down the dusty road, suddenly on my left, was the same deserted road that I had been down before. By this time, it was already getting dark, but I had traveled this far to find out the truth, so there was no turning back now.

Before turning in, I checked all my gauges to make sure everything looked good, because the last thing I needed was for this rental to break down at the very end of the road. With a deep breathe, I turned in and made my way down the narrow dirt road. About a quarter mile down, was this big beautiful tree, that looks like it has stood at the entry to the valley for many years. And to the left of the tree, I could see a full moon, starting to rise but for some reason, this felt different in a way that I can't explain. As I approached the tree, there was some sort of light coming from behind it. It wasn't really noticeable, but something that I had not noticed before, and I was not going to stop to investigate. I only wanted to make it to the dead end, to see if I noticed anything, and then get the hell out of there before it got too late. I did look in my rearview mirror to see if I could spot anything, but nothing was there. A few minutes later, I arrived to the end of the road where I had found the guillotine at originally, I put the car in park and stepped out to stretch my legs and smoke a cigarette before heading back to the waterfall.

It was getting late and I was starting to feel exhausted from the long trip from Houston, plus I had already seen everything that I needed to see for the day. Hopefully, I could make it back to town with no problems and find a decent room with a hot shower, and a comfortable bed.

After I finished smoking my cigarette, I hurried back to the car so that I could get off this old abandoned road. As I approached the tree on the way out, there was a young man in his twenties walking along the brush. I didn't remember seeing him when I drove in, and I knew for a fact that he wasn't there. As I got closer, he turned to looked at me, and I could see that it was William.

On the way back to town, at mile marker eighteen, I saw him again. Only this time, he was standing in the middle of the street holding the camera with one hand and pointing with his left hand. I had no choice but to stop and see what he was pointing at. A few feet from the road was a mile marker that had a pink tape wrapped around it, and it did not look new either. But for some reason, something told me to get out and go see for myself, what he was trying to show me. At this point, I was not scared anymore, and for some reason, that I did not know, I felt as though I was a part of him.

We were standing face to face in the middle of the road, and I could tell that he was just like the little girl and the two sisters that I had met before. He was a ghost, and on his shirt, the name tag said W. F. Vermillion. The Jeep was still running, with the headlights to my back when the soldier slowly turned around and started walking out towards the middle of the field. He must have been about twenty feet away from me, when he turned around and waved, before disappearing into the night.

At that moment I knew why, I was called back to this place, there was only one thing left to do, and that was to wait for my calling.

# CHAPTER THIRTEEN

## *Headed Home*

The next morning as I drove away from that waterfall, I could feel something inside of me. It was a feeling that I had not felt in a while. A feeling of closure, knowing that this adventure was almost complete. It was God who called me to this place and sent his angels to guide me to the truth.

After a few miles, I noticed the sun starting to come up in front of me. Without a doubt, I knew that I was driving east, but still wanted to double check myself to make sure my phone was working, and it was.

The sky was clear, the air was fresh, and I felt a sense of relief, knowing that I could finally go home and see my family. It has been almost six months living in the mountains, bathing in the creek, and sleeping under the stars. But the feeling I felt driving away from that waterfall told me that my mission was complete. I have accomplished what I set out to do, and that was *Finding Fenn's Treasure.*

I know my life will forever be changed knowing that I am the one who held the keys to this treasure hunt. And as far as my new friends at the waterfall, I am sure I will be back one day to visit with them and see if they need any help getting things ready for their new visitors. Because sometimes people overlook what is there, not everyone can see the real treasure that lies in that area. So why do the yellow and purple flowers flourish where no one is there to see? Does anyone have to be there to see when the grass sees, the trees, and the rushing water of the spring creek also see? And now I see the beauty in that place that no one else could see. I see the ones that are there, pruning the flowers, pulling the weeds, and I can see her, Anna Karen Valdez watering the flowers. She helped me find her stone marker that night in eighteen-degree water and kept me warm throughout the night.

So now, it is my responsibility to stand at the head of the valley and help those lost souls who venture to that place. I will continue to help them to understand that their lives amongst the living was not waisted. And that while they were here, they served a purpose, whether it was to cause a smile on someone's face, or even to enrich the lives of others.

So now I know who I am. I am a father, a son, a husband, and a Texas Patriot. But most importantly, I am also an angel of God, who answered his call to venture into a place that I had never been before to walk in the valley of death and save someone's life.

# Closure

Forrest Fenn achieved what he set out to do. He wanted to find that one person who would seek the truth in his treasure hunt. It was not all about finding gold at the end of the rainbow, it was more about finding that one person he never expected to exist. And in his venture, he wished to have enriched the lives of many, by doing something that no one has ever done before. And from one treasure hunter to another, I think he had accomplished what he set out to do.

If you are ever in the area of Browns Park, and decide to venture towards Vermillion Waterfalls, the aluminum grave marker he placed in the valley, still stands in the same spot that he had placed it over 10 years ago. During the month of March and early April at 17:55, if you are standing at the aluminum marker, you will have the chance to see The Blaze. Also take some time some time to locate the stone marker that sits in the middle of the creek. The directions are in his book. And as for The Blaze that everyone has been searching for, it can only be seen for about 30-45 minutes every day before the sun eventually disappears behind the mountains for the night. If you are wise, right below The Blaze, sits his special place, the place that he had wanted his bones to remain undiscovered for a million years.

I know this location may be confidential and personal to him, which I do know why. But since Fenn has chosen to leave it up to the finder, as to whether or not the location will remain Pristine. I have decided that everyone should have the same opportunity to be a part of history and witness the magic for themselves.

It was God's shadow that night standing next to me, and he sent his Angels to protect me. And one Angel in particular was Anna Karen Valdez Ramirez. She is the Homely Girl that held onto my hand and she never let go. **Forrest Fenn I have the Title to your Gold.**

# Home of Brown

## Baptiste Brown

Others believe that a **French-Canadian trapper** by the name of **Baptiste Brown** is the rightful claimant. One writer claim that "Two years after Ashley's visit...**Baptiste Brown,** wandered into the Hole," and "did something a voyageur rarely did; that is, he decided to settle down. Choosing a site not far from the confluence of **Vermillion Creek** and the **Greene River,** he built a cabin for himself and his Blackfoot squaw." Another account says that Baptiste Brown was one of Henry Fraeb's men and had participated in the last pitched battle between Indians and trappers on the **Little Snake River,** just east of Brown's Hole.

The town of Flagler on Colorado's Eastern Plains was the scene of one of the worst air show crashes in U.S. history.

Twenty people — 13 of them children — were killed on Sept. 15, 1951 when a single engine plane hooked a wing while doing a maneuver and careened into a crowd of more than 1,000 people who had gathered from all around the area to see the show, sponsored by the Flagler Lions Club as a highlight of Fall Festival Day.

Another 50 people were injured. The pilot, 1st Lt. Norman Jones from Lowry Air Force Base, was among the dead.

# Butch Cassidy

Robert LeRoy Parker was born on April 13, 1866 in Beaver, Utah, the first of 13 children of British immigrants Maximillian Parker and Ann Campbell Gillies.

Parker fled his home as a teenager and while working on a dairy ranch he met Mike Cassidy, a horse and cattle thief. He subsequently worked on several ranches, in addition to a brief apprenticeship with a butcher in Rock Springs, Wyoming, where he got the nickname (by the word "butcher," which morphed later into "Butch"), to which he soon added the last name Cassidy in honor of his old friend and mentor.

# Thirteen to Be Exact

A 13-year-old Stephenville girl is dead, the victim of drowning in a river in the northwestern corner of Colorado.

Karen Valdez was found Monday morning in the Yampa River - not wearing a life jacket - after last being seen swimming about 6 p.m. Sunday.

The accident occurred in the Yampa River near Craig, Colo., a town of about 10,000 about 40 miles from Steamboat Springs and in the vicinity of the Colorado and Wyoming border.

"Our victim slipped and kind of slid in a hole," Jantz told the Daily Press. "She grabbed a cousin. The cousin stood up, and they saw the victim go under the water. That was the last they saw her, which was about 10 minutes prior to the time they called us.

# Timothy H O'Sullivan

We also know when the Civil War began in early 1861, he was commissioned a first lieutenant in the Union Army. There is no record of him fighting. Alexander Gardner worked as a photographer on the staff of General George B. McClellan, commander of the Army of the Potomac, and was given the honorary rank of captain. Gardner described O'Sullivan as the "Superintendent of my map and field work." Biographer James D. Horan writes that O'Sullivan was a civilian photographer attached to the Topographical

Engineers. His job was to copy maps and plans, but he also took photographs on his own time. Although he later listed himself as a first lieutenant, the rank was likely honorary, like Gardner's.

# William F Vermillion

**Nationality**
American
**Nickname**
Not yet known
**Service numbers**
37128367
**Highest Rank**
Staff Sergeant
**Role/job**
Radio Operator
**Awards**

- European-African-Middle Eastern Campaign Medal
- Prisoner of War Medal
- World War II Victory Medal

Assigned to 455BS, 323BG, 9AF USAAF. 30 x missions. Failed to Return (FTR) mission to V-1 target near Devres, FR a direct flak hit near the left engine forced crew to bail-out. Prisoner of War (POW). MACR 2056.

# Joseph Lafayette Meek

Joseph Lafayette "Joe" Meek

Joseph was a pioneer, mountain man, law enforcement official, and politician in the Oregon Country and later Oregon Territory of the United States. A trapper involved in the fur trade before settling in the Tualatin Valley, Meek played a prominent role at the Champoeg Meetings of 1843, where he was elected a sheriff. He was later elected to and served in the Provisional Legislature of Oregon before being appointed as the United States Marshal for the Oregon Territory.

# Josie Bassett

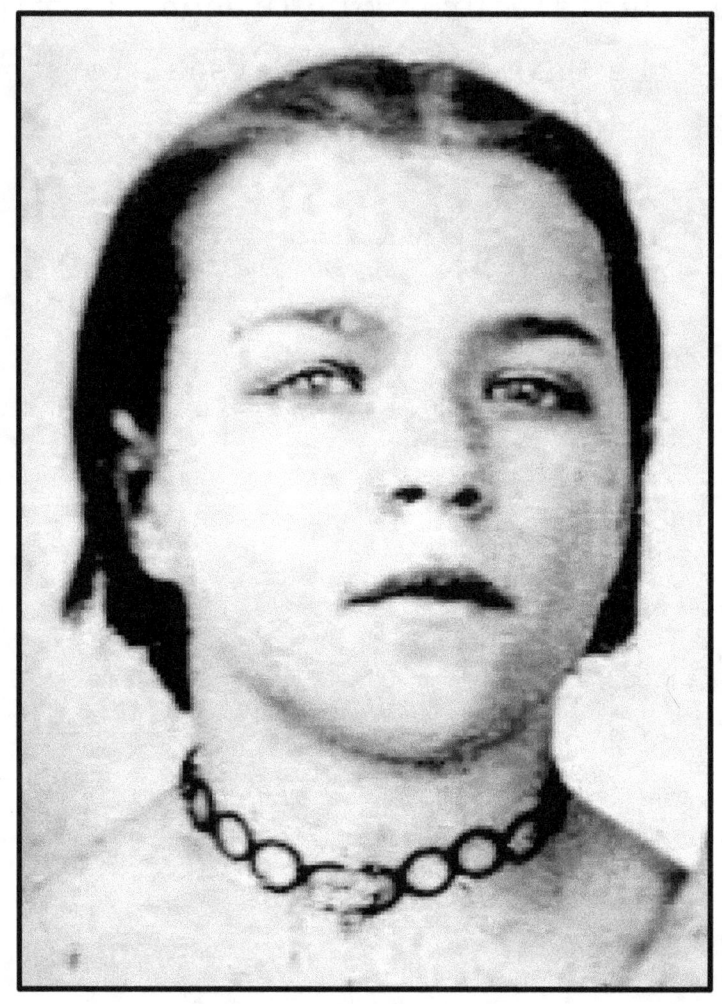

Josie Bassett was born the first of two girls to Herb Bassett and Mary Eliza Chamberlain (Elizabeth) Bassett in Arkansas on January 17, 1874. When she was still a young girl, her parents moved to a ranch spanning the borders of Utah, Wyoming and Colorado.

She and her sister were taught to rope, ride, and shoot at a young age. Both girls were sent to prominent boarding schools in their youth, but both chose to return to the ranching life by their teen years.

# Ann Bassett

Bassett was born to Herb Bassett and Elizabeth Chamberlain Bassett near Browns Park, Colorado, but grew up in Utah, the second of two daughters. Her sister Josie was born in 1874. Herb Bassett was twenty years senior to his wife Elizabeth Chamberlain Bassett, and the couple moved to Browns Park sometime around the earlier part of 1888. Herb

Bassett had a profitable cattle ranch which straddled Utah, Wyoming, and Colorado.

# Conclusion

In the process of trying to figure everything out so that it all flows together, many searchers failed to do one major thing before driving across country to search for Fenn's Treasure. They failed to buy his book, TTOTC.

After purchasing his book, I slowly started to realize that everything was either a clue or riddle. And in the process, Mr. Fenn managed to tell an awesome story that many of the treasure hunters could not comprehend.

When Mr. Fenn tells his audience, *to think like a child*, he meant do what a child would do. And kids enjoy playing at the park. Forrest spent a lot of time at Brown's Park setting up a huge treasure hunt, for adults to play. He wanted to get adults off their computers and phones and get them back into nature and moving again.

The photos in TTOTC, all have a meaning. They represent a time in history about events that have occurred in the past. These events may not have been important as other events documented in history books, but Forrest knows that they can never be forgotten.

So, if you are ever at the park, and feel like you are ready for an adventure, and want to learn the story for yourself. Then get up and get out there with your family and make lasting memories. Because at the end of the day, all that we really leave behind is a memory.

As for me, I will be working on a special project, because someone had to take the lead for the treasure hunt. And that night by the waterfall, I was handed the key to the next chapter of this treasure hunt.

The Chase Will Continue...

www.ingramcontent.com/pod-product-compliance
Lightning Source LLC
Chambersburg PA
CBHW08081725 0626
47159CB00010B/3416